Race Ahead with Reading

Pirates are Stealing our COWS

By Martin Remphry

W
FRANKLIN WATTS
LONDON•SYDNEY

Pirates really did steal three
Guernsey cows from the
Channel Island of Brecqhou.

But what did pirates want
with cows?

For Zack Perrée – M.R.

Chapter 1

"Pirates are stealing our cows!"
spluttered Farmer Marchant.

Mrs Marchant looked up from her tea.
"What would pirates want with cows?"
she wondered.

Farmer Marchant dropped his toast and
ran down to the beach in his slippers.

But Daisy, Buttercup and
Milkshake were already
sailing away from the tiny
island, with their
stripy-shirted captors
waving cutlasses
in the air.

Mrs Marchant poured herself a fresh cup of tea and telephoned the police.

"I would like to report the theft of our cows by pirates. They are called Daisy, Buttercup and Milkshake."

"Funny names for pirates," said the officer.

"Daisy, Buttercup and Milkshake are our

cows!" snapped Mrs Marchant.

"Whatever their names, pirates don't steal

cows. They steal treasure. Anyway, if we

tried to arrest them, our cars would sink,"

the officer snapped back.

Farmer Marchant stomped into the kitchen and shook the sand from his slippers.

"I'll go after those cow-stealing sea dogs myself!" he growled, whisking the tablecloth from under the teapot.

Farmer Marchant dragged a cattle trough to the beach. He tied the tablecloth up as a sail. Mrs Marchant handed him some sandwiches and pushed him out into the waves.

"Make sure you bring them back in time for milking," she called as he paddled with his spade out to sea.

Chapter 2

The captain peered down at
the cattle trough bobbing
beside his battleship.

"What are you
doing sailing in
a cattle trough?"
he called.
"Looking for my
cows," replied
Farmer Marchant.
"They were stolen
by pirates!"

"Pirates don't steal cows. They only steal baboons," shouted the captain.

"Don't you mean doubloons?" asked the farmer.

"Pirates have treasure chests stuffed full of baboons. It says so in all the storybooks. Anyway, I'm far too busy hunting submarines to go chasing after pirates."

Farmer Marchant watched the battleship disappear over the horizon.

Crunch! A submarine's periscope rose up through the bottom of the cattle trough.

Farmer Marchant peered into the metal tube.

"Has anyone down there seen any pirates with cows?" he called.

"Pirates don't have cows," said a voice from below. "They have parrots. Cows would fall off their shoulders. Anyway, we're on the lookout for battleships, not pirates."

"Well, unless I repair this hole, I'm coming to the bottom of the sea with you. Can you drop me off on that island over there?" asked Farmer Marchant.

Chapter 3

Farmer Marchant watched the submarine

sink back under the waves.

Moooooo!

The farmer spun around. Eating grass under a palm tree stood Daisy, Buttercup and Milkshake.

Behind them fidgeted three very embarrassed pirates with their ship stuck in the sand.

"Well?" asked Farmer Marchant, crossing his arms. "Why did you steal my cows?" One pirate shuffled his wooden leg. "We ran out of milk and Captain Sprat was thirsty," he mumbled.

"But we're not very good at milking."

The pirates showed their silver hook hands.

"We were so busy trying to fill the Captain's bowl that we didn't see the island ahead."

"And who is Captain Sprat?" asked Farmer Marchant.

One of the pirates handed Farmer Marchant a small black and white kitten.

"Captain Sprat is the ship's cat," mumbled the pirates.

Chapter 4

The pirates were truly sorry that they had stolen Daisy, Buttercup and Milkshake, and promised to make it up to the farmer and to Mrs Marchant.

Once they had dug the pirate ship out of the sand everyone sailed back to the farm.

As soon as they landed, Mrs Marchant put the pirates to work. She gave their grubby pirate clothes to the scarecrow and handed them pitchforks and clean overalls.

Flinty Sharp mucked out the pigsty.

Scratch'em Matchan collected the eggs.

Crusher Chesney dug the potatoes.

"Breakfast!" called Mrs Marchant from the kitchen door, banging a large frying pan with her wooden spoon.

Chapter Five

"A farmer's breakfast is much nicer than a pirate's," munched Flinty Sharp, buttering himself a seventh slice of toast with his cutlass. "All we get are sardines and ship's biscuits."

"And you don't feel seasick while you're eating it," added Crusher Chesney.

"I quite like being a farmer," said
Scratch'em Matchan. "Can you teach me
how to sail your tractor?"

"You'll have plenty of time to learn," said
Mrs Marchant, scooping more fried eggs
onto their plates. "It looks like someone is
stealing your ship!"

The pirates dropped their toast and eggs
and scrambled down to the beach, just in
time to see their ship being sailed away by
three rather unusual pirates.

"Looks like Daisy, Buttercup and Milkshake got a taste for the pirate life!" laughed Farmer Marchant.

First published in 2013 by
Franklin Watts
338 Euston Road
London
NW1 3BH

Franklin Watts Australia
Level 17/207 Kent Street
Sydney
NSW 2000

Text and illustration © Martin Remphry 2013

The rights of Martin Remphry to be
identified as the author and illustrator
of this Work have been asserted in
accordance with the Copyright, Designs
and Patents Act, 1988.

Series Editor: Melanie Palmer
Editor: Jackie Hamley
Series Advisor: Catherine Glavina
Series Designer: Peter Scoulding

A CIP catalogue record for this book is
available from the British Library.

ISBN 978 1 4451 2642 5 (hbk)
ISBN 978 1 4451 2648 7 (pbk)
ISBN 978 1 4451 2660 9 (library ebook)

Printed in China

Franklin Watts is a division of Hachette
Children's Books, an Hachette UK company.
www.hachette.co.uk